How the Sun Got to Coco's House

To my son Pete.
Ever an artist and
always an inspiration to me.

First published 2015 by Walker Books Ltd
87 Vauxhall Walk, London SE11 5HJ

This edition published 2017

10 9 8 7 6 5 4 3 2 1

This book has been typeset in Garamond Ludlow

Printed in China

British Library Cataloguing in Publication Data:
a catalogue record for this book is available from the British Library

ISBN 978-1-4063-7345-5

www.walker.co.uk

Amnesty International UK endorses this book because
it reminds us that this world belongs to all of us and
we all have the right to enjoy life, freedom and safety.

WALKER BOOKS
AND SUBSIDIARIES
LONDON · BOSTON · SYDNEY · AUCKLAND

How the Sun
Got to Coco's House

BOB GRAHAM

It had to start somewhere.

While Coco slept faraway, the sun crept up slowly behind a hill, paused for a moment, seemed to think twice ...

before it plunged down the other side and skidded giddy across the water.

It touched a fisherman's cap and with help from the wind ...

blew it off!

The sun tumbled end over end.
It was caught briefly in the eye of a whale ...

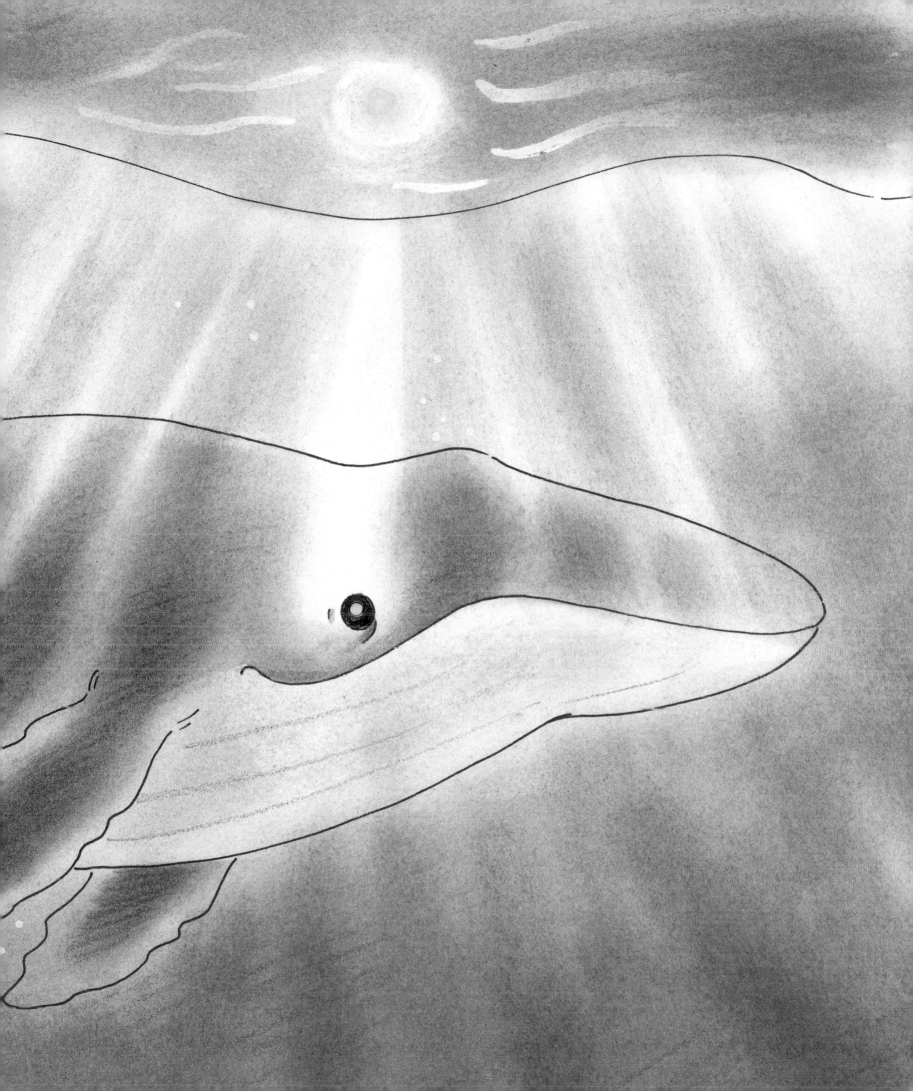

then headed up the beach

and out over frozen forests, making shadows on the snow

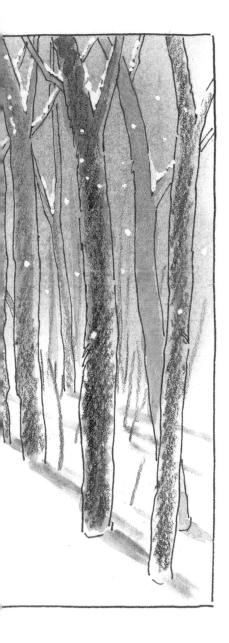

and in Jung Su's footsteps.

The rising sun met birds still flying south for the winter
and a plane flying high in the night.

It balanced out on the wing –
just for young Lovejoy, off to visit his grandma.

It crossed a city, took a short cut down a laneway

and waited patiently outside an old lady's window to be let in.

The sun took off over the countryside,

woke bears

and snow cats

and caught Kosha and his father
on their way to market.

High over a desert,

it met the rain.

Over the mountains, in a small village,
Alika's toe broke ice in a puddle.

Then the sun leapt
whole countries,
chasing the night.

It lit the East Side of a city and took
passing glances at itself in office towers.

Bold as you like,
it extinguished
the street lights
on Coco's street.

It briefly trapped itself in
the paper boy's bell.

Then ...

the winter sun barged straight through Coco's window!

It followed her down the hall,

made itself quite at home on her mum and dad's bed

and joined them for breakfast.

After such a dash, the sun had time on its hands. So did Coco!

So did Coco's friends!

But for a few passing clouds,

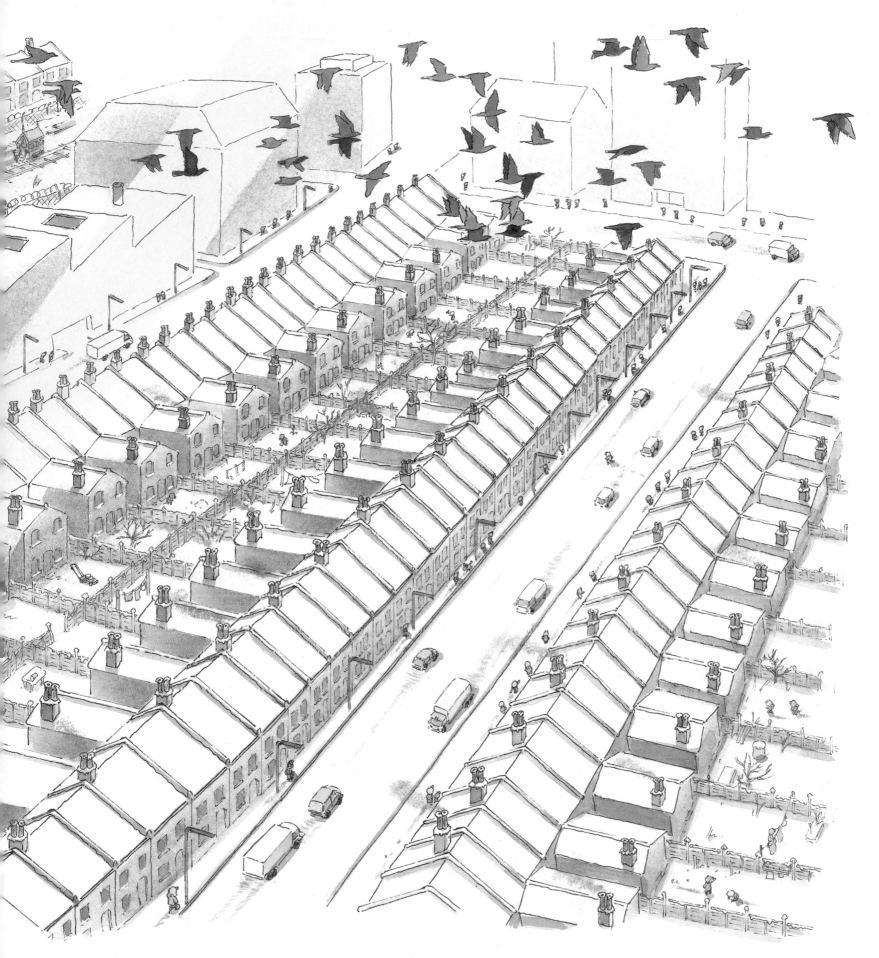

they spent the whole day together.